STAR WARS
THE RISE OF SKYWALKER
WARS
AMAZING STICKER ADVENTURES

HOW TO USE THIS BOOK

Read the captions, then find
the sticker that best fits the space.
(Hint: check the sticker labels for clues!)

•

There are lots of fantastic extra
stickers for creating your
own scenes!

DK | Penguin Random House

Written by David Fentiman
Designer Chris Gould
Pre-production Producer Marc Staples
Senior Producer Mary Slater
Managing Editor Sadie Smith
Managing Art Editor Vicky Short
Publisher Julie Ferris
Art Director Lisa Lanzarini
Publishing Director Simon Beecroft

For Lucasfilm
Senior Editor Brett Rector
Creative Director of Publishing Michael Siglain
Art Director Troy Alders
Story Group James Waugh, Pablo Hidalgo,
Leland Chee, and Matt Martin

First American Edition, 2019
Published in the United States by DK Publishing
1450 Broadway, Suite 801, New York, NY 10018

Page design copyright © 2019 Dorling Kindersley Limited
DK, a Division of Penguin Random House LLC
19 20 21 22 23 10 9 8 7 6 5 4 3 2 1
001–311515–Oct/2019

Published in Great Britain by Dorling Kindersley Limited.

A catalog record for this book is available from the Library of Congress.

ISBN: 978-1-4654-7904-4

DK books are available at special discounts when purchased in bulk for sales promotions,
premiums, fund-raising, or educational use. For details, contact:
DK Publishing Special Markets, 1450 Broadway, Suite 801, New York, NY 10018
SpecialSales@dk.com

Printed and bound in China

A WORLD OF IDEAS:
SEE ALL THERE IS TO KNOW

www.dk.com
www.starwars.com

REY
Resistance hero and Jedi warrior

Hair tied up for battle

DATA FILE

SPECIES: Human
AFFILIATION: Resistance, Jedi
ABILITIES: Force abilities, lightsaber combat, piloting
WEAPONS: Lightsaber

REY is heroic and compassionate. She will learn the ways of the **JEDI** to defeat Kylo Ren.

Arm band

Jedi belt

Lightsaber

Bracer

KYLO REN
Supreme Leader of the First Order

KYLO REN is evil and powerful. He leads the **FIRST ORDER**. Kylo wants to destroy Rey and the Resistance.

Lightsaber blade

Mask

Cloak

Lightsaber crossblade

Padded armor

DATA FILE

SPECIES: Human
AFFILIATION: First Order, Knights of Ren
ABILITIES: Force abilities, lightsaber combat
WEAPONS: Lightsaber

SUPREME LEADER

Kylo Ren and the First Order have conquered nearly the entire galaxy! Only the Resistance can stop him.

KYLO'S FORCES
The Supreme Leader commands many armies

STORMTROOPERS
First Order soldiers are called stormtroopers. They all look identical and have numbers instead of names.

SITH TROOPERS
Kylo has an army of elite stormtroopers. They all wear intimidating suits of red armor.

TIE FIGHTERS
The First Order's TIE fighters take on the Resistance's ships in space battles.

THE KNIGHTS OF REN
The six Knights of Ren are Kylo's most powerful warriors. They wear masks and carry unique weapons.

REY'S ALLIES

Many heroes have joined the Resistance

FINN
Brave Finn is Rey's closest friend. He is smart, tough, and determined to fight the First Order.

CHEWBACCA
Chewie is a Wookiee from the planet Kashyyyk. He is loyal and brave, and a skilled mechanic.

D-O
D-O is an excitable little droid who was put together using spare parts. He wants to be just like his droid friend, BB-8.

POE
Poe is the best pilot in the Resistance. He can fly starships better than anyone else in the galaxy.

JANNAH
Jannah is a fierce warrior from an ocean moon. She is fast and athletic, and she can shoot her energy bow with great skill.

Rey's friends in the Resistance all look up to her. They know that she can defeat Kylo Ren and save the galaxy.

JANNAH
Fierce freedom fighter

JANNAH is tough and brave. She leads a band of noble warriors against the evil **FIRST ORDER.**

Goggles

Finger guard

Energy bow

Grappling hook

Strong grip

DATA FILE

SPECIES: Human
AFFILIATION: Resistance-allied
ABILITIES: Archery, riding
WEAPONS: Energy bow, grapple hook

SITH TROOPER

Elite First Order soldiers

SITH TROOPERS are the First Order's most powerful soldiers. They are inspired by **THE DARK SIDE**.

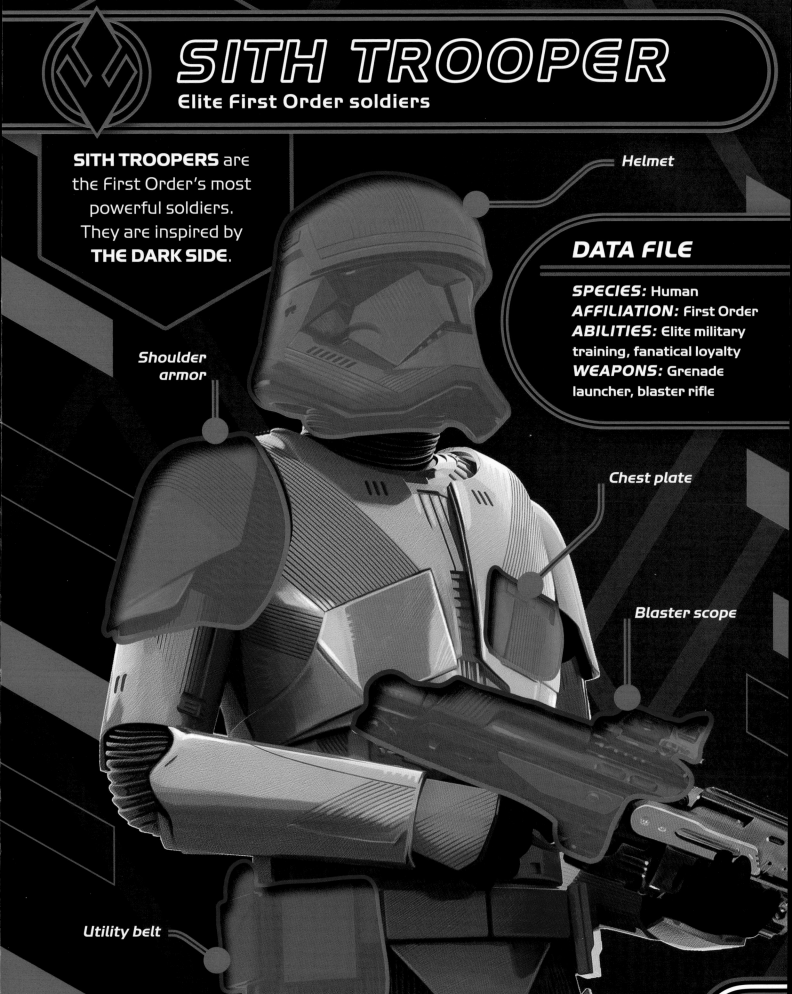

Helmet

Shoulder armor

Chest plate

Blaster scope

Utility belt

DATA FILE

SPECIES: Human
AFFILIATION: First Order
ABILITIES: Elite military training, fanatical loyalty
WEAPONS: Grenade launcher, blaster rifle

THE FIRST ORDER

The soldiers of the First Order want to conquer the galaxy!

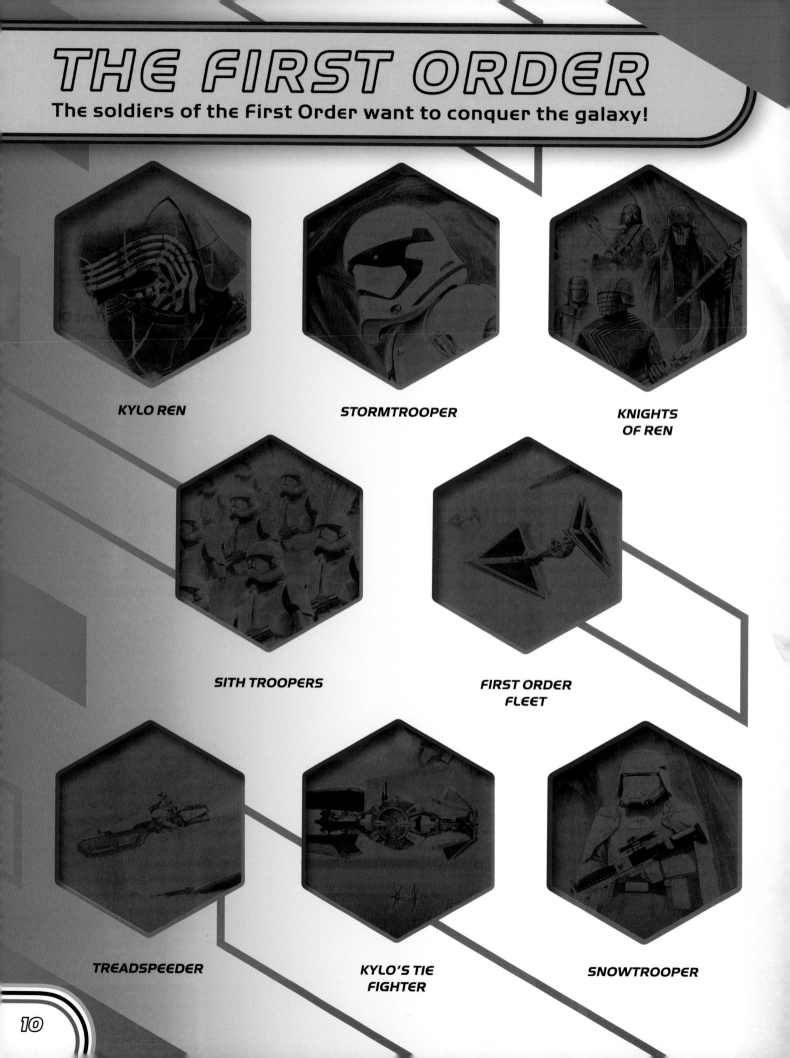

KYLO REN

STORMTROOPER

KNIGHTS
OF REN

SITH TROOPERS

FIRST ORDER
FLEET

TREADSPEEDER

KYLO'S TIE
FIGHTER

SNOWTROOPER

THE RESISTANCE

Rey's friends must defend the galaxy!

REY

MILLENNIUM FALCON

BB-8 AND D-O

PASAANA SPEEDERS

FINN AND JANNAH

POE

C-3PO AND R2-D2

X-WINGS

LANDO AND CHEWBACCA

TOP 3: DROIDS

C-3PO

Choose your three **FAVORITE DROIDS** and then add their stickers!

R2-D2

3

BB-8

D-O

1

2

RESISTANCE SHIPS

Speedy fighters and powerful bombers

RESISTANCE X-WINGS

T-70 X-wings are the most common Resistance starfighters. They are fast and are powerfully armed. Their four wings open out into an X shape.

A-WINGS

A-wings are the Resistance's fastest fighters. They can zoom into battle and easily outrun enemy ships.

Y-WINGS

Y-wings are slow but powerful bomber ships. They are quite old fashioned, but the Resistance uses an upgraded version.

MILLENNIUM FALCON

The *Millennium Falcon*'s quad laser turrets make it a deadly ship in any space battle. First Order pilots fear the mighty *Falcon*!

POE'S X-WING

Poe leads the other Resistance pilots into battle. His unique X-wing has a colorful paint job, so everyone can see where he is.

TOP 3: TIE FIGHTERS

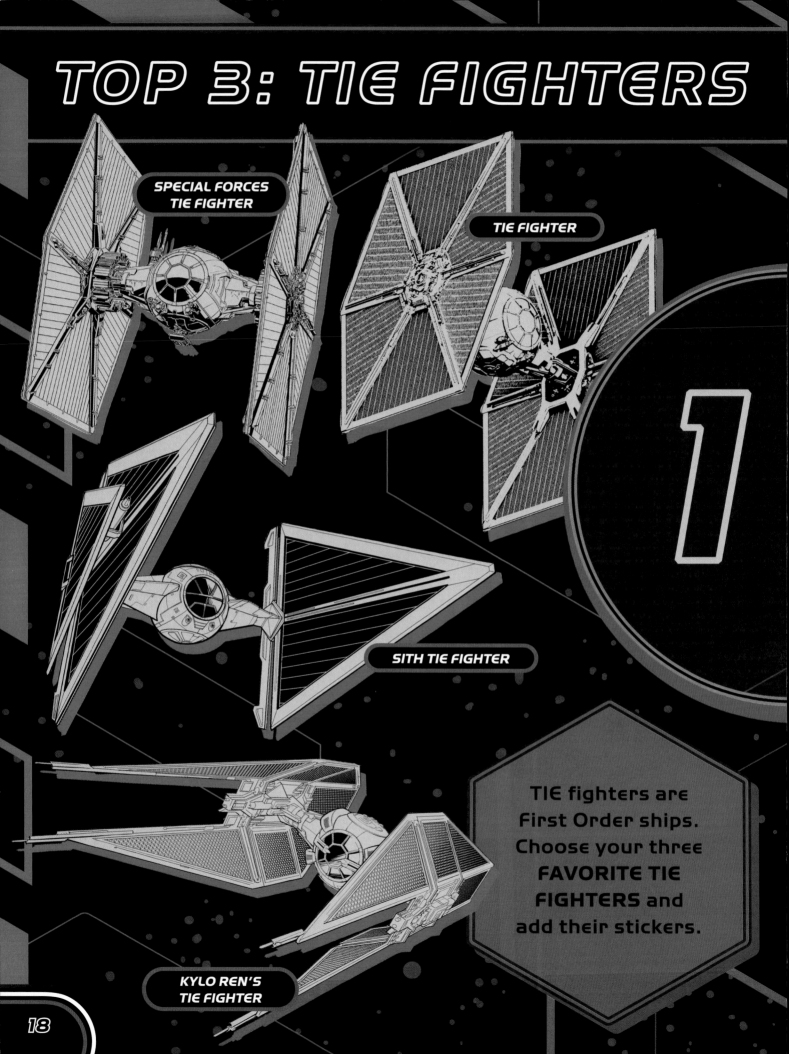

SPECIAL FORCES TIE FIGHTER

TIE FIGHTER

1

SITH TIE FIGHTER

TIE fighters are First Order ships. Choose your three **FAVORITE TIE FIGHTERS** and add their stickers.

KYLO REN'S TIE FIGHTER

MILLENNIUM FALCON

Legendary Resistance starship

Cockpit

Shield generator

Maintenance bay

The **MILLENNIUM FALCON** is Chewbacca's starship. It is one of the fastest ships in the galaxy.

Laser cannon turret

DATA FILE

AFFILIATION: Resistance
LENGTH: 35 meters (115 feet)
CREW: Two (standard)
WEAPONS: Two quad laser cannons, ground-sweeper laser cannon, concussion missile launchers

Forward mandible

Missile bay

Use your EXTRA STICKERS to fill the Millennium Falcon!

ZORII
Leader of the Spice Runners

Helmet

ZORII is tough and streetsmart. Although she is a **CRIME BOSS**, Zorii must choose if she will join a side in the war.

DATA FILE

SPECIES: Human
AFFILIATION: Spice Runners of Kijimi
ABILITIES: Piloting, ranged combat, close combat
WEAPONS: Twin blaster pistols

Arm bands

Belt

Gauntlet

Blaster pistol

SNOWTROOPER
Cold weather stormtrooper

On **ICY WORLDS** the First Order uses its **SNOWTROOPERS.** Their special armor keeps them warm.

Helmet

Blaster scope

Blaster barrel

Knee guard

Utility pouch

DATA FILE

SPECIES: Human
AFFILIATION: First Order
ABILITIES: Cold weather training, ranged combat
WEAPONS: Blaster rifle

THE KNIGHTS OF REN

Kylo Ren's mysterious allies

**KNIGHT OF REN
(BLASTER RIFLE)**

**KNIGHT OF REN
(LONG AX)**

**KNIGHT OF REN
(SCYTHE)**

**KNIGHT OF REN
(HEAVY BLADE)**

**KNIGHT OF REN
(WAR CLUB)**

**KNIGHT OF REN
(ARM CANNON)**

MASKED WARRIORS

Each Knight of Ren carries a unique weapon and wears a mask. They show no fear and are almost unbeatable in battle.

LANDO
Legendary rebel leader

Many years ago, **LANDO CALRISSIAN** was a **REBEL HERO**. Now the Resistance must ask him for help.

Styled hair

DATA FILE

SPECIES: Human
AFFILIATION: Resistance-allied
ABILITIES: Ranged combat, negotiation
WEAPONS: Staff, blaster pistol

Colorful shirt

Cane

Holstered blaster

Cape

KNIGHT OF REN
Supreme Leader's enforcer

Helmet

DATA FILE

SPECIES: Unknown
AFFILIATION: First Order
ABILITIES: Physical combat
WEAPONS: Club staff, thermal detonators

Club staff

Thermal detonators

Gauntlet

Mud-splattered robe

The six **KNIGHTS OF REN** are fearsome warriors. They hide their faces beneath **SCARY MASKS**.

RESISTANCE X-WING

Backbone of the Resistance fleet

Engine

Astromech droid

Wing

Laser cannon

X-WINGS are much stronger than the First Order's **TIE FIGHTERS**, but there aren't very many of them.

Nose cone

DATA FILE

AFFILIATION: Resistance
LENGTH: 12.7 meters (42 feet)
CREW: One pilot
WEAPONS: Four laser cannons, proton torpedoes

Use your **EXTRA STICKERS** to fill the hyperspace tunnel!

STICKERS FOR REY

Hair tied up for battle

Jedi belt

Bracer

Arm band

Lightsaber

STICKERS FOR KYLO REN

Cloak

Lightsaber blade

Mask

Lightsaber crossblade

Padded armor

STICKERS FOR JANNAH

Finger guard

Strong grip

Grappling hook

Energy bow

Goggles

STICKERS FOR SITH TROOPER

Utility belt

Blaster scope

Shoulder armor

Helmet

Chest plate

STICKERS FOR KYLO'S FORCES

Sith troopers

TIE fighters

Stormtroopers

The Knights of Ren

EXTRA STICKERS

EXTRA STICKERS

STICKERS FOR REY'S ALLIES

Poe

Chewbacca

Finn

D-O

Jannah

STICKERS FOR THE FIRST ORDER

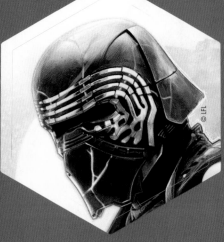

Kylo Ren

Knights of Ren

Stormtrooper

Sith troopers

First Order fleet

Kylo's TIE fighter

Treadspeeder

Snowtrooper

STICKERS FOR THE RESISTANCE

Rey

BB-8 and D-O

Millennium Falcon

Pasaana speeders

Finn and Jannah

Poe

C-3PO and R2-D2

X-wings

Lando and Chewbacca

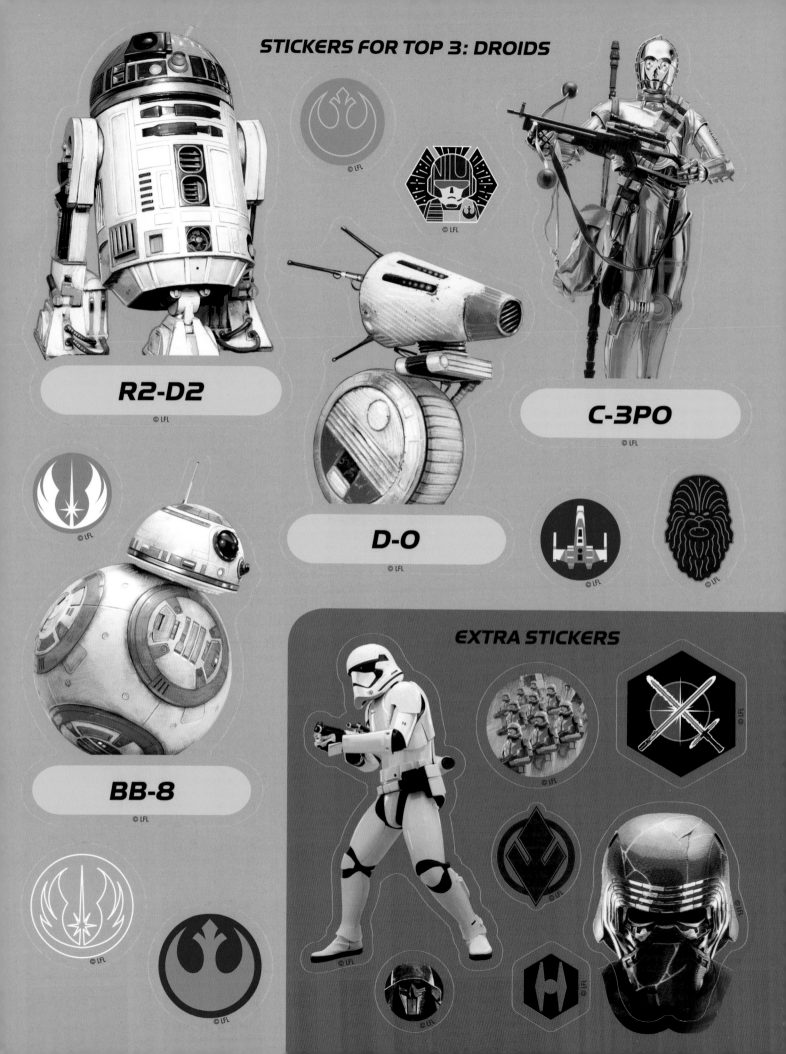

STICKERS FOR TOP 3: DROIDS

R2-D2

C-3PO

D-O

BB-8

EXTRA STICKERS

EXTRA STICKERS

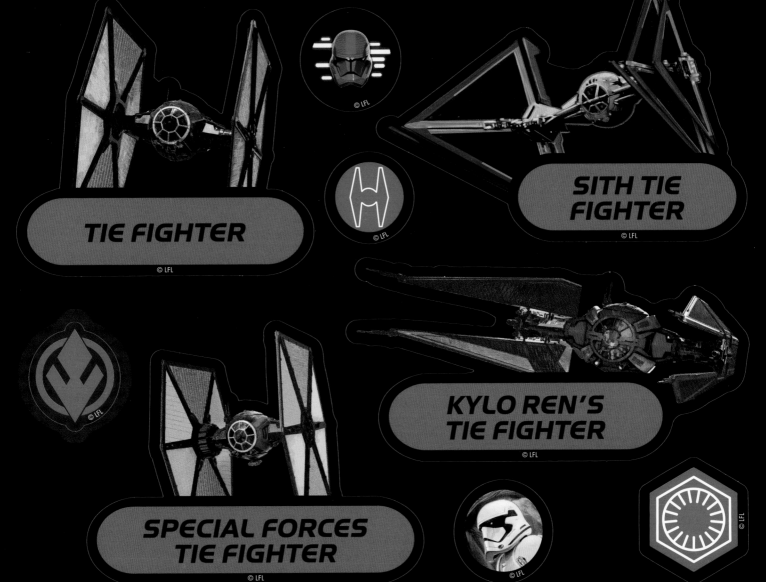

STICKERS FOR TOP 3: TIE FIGHTERS

TIE FIGHTER

SITH TIE FIGHTER

KYLO REN'S TIE FIGHTER

SPECIAL FORCES TIE FIGHTER

STICKERS FOR RESISTANCE SHIPS

A-wings

Millennium Falcon

Y-wings

Poe's X-wing

EXTRA STICKERS

EXTRA STICKERS

STICKERS FOR THE KNIGHTS OF REN

Knight of Ren (blaster rifle)

Knight of Ren (long ax)

Knight of Ren (war club)

Knight of Ren (arm cannon)

Knight of Ren (heavy blade)

Knight of Ren (scythe)

STICKERS FOR MILLENNIUM FALCON

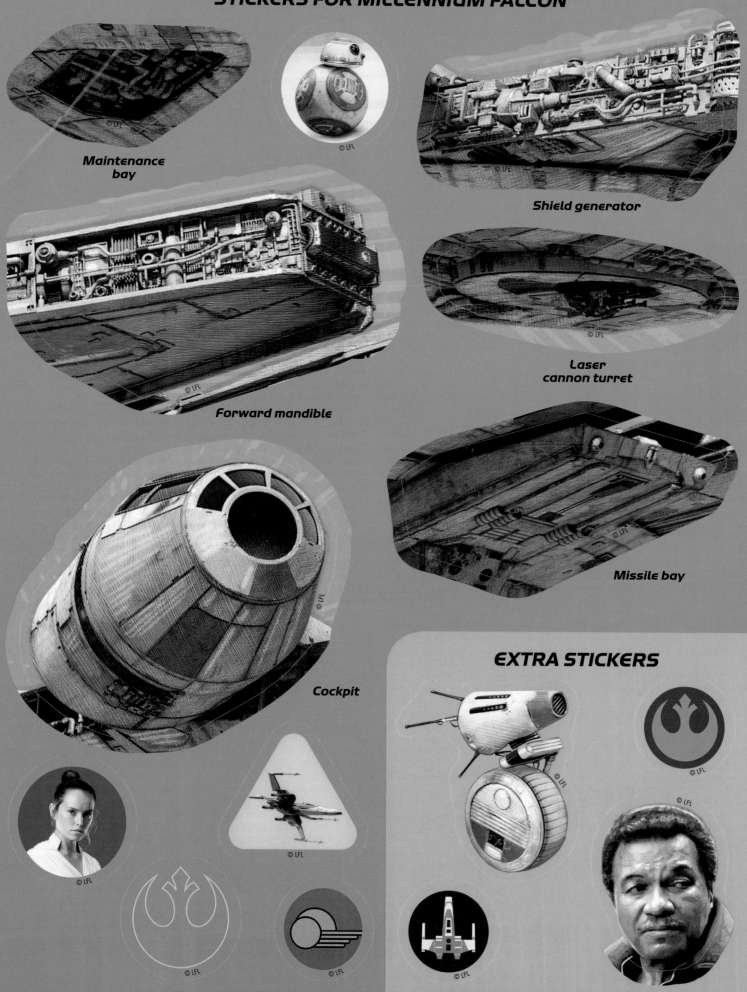

Maintenance bay

Shield generator

Forward mandible

Laser cannon turret

Missile bay

Cockpit

EXTRA STICKERS

EXTRA STICKERS

STICKERS FOR X-WING

Laser cannon

Astromech droid

Engine

Wing

Nose cone

STICKERS FOR ZORII

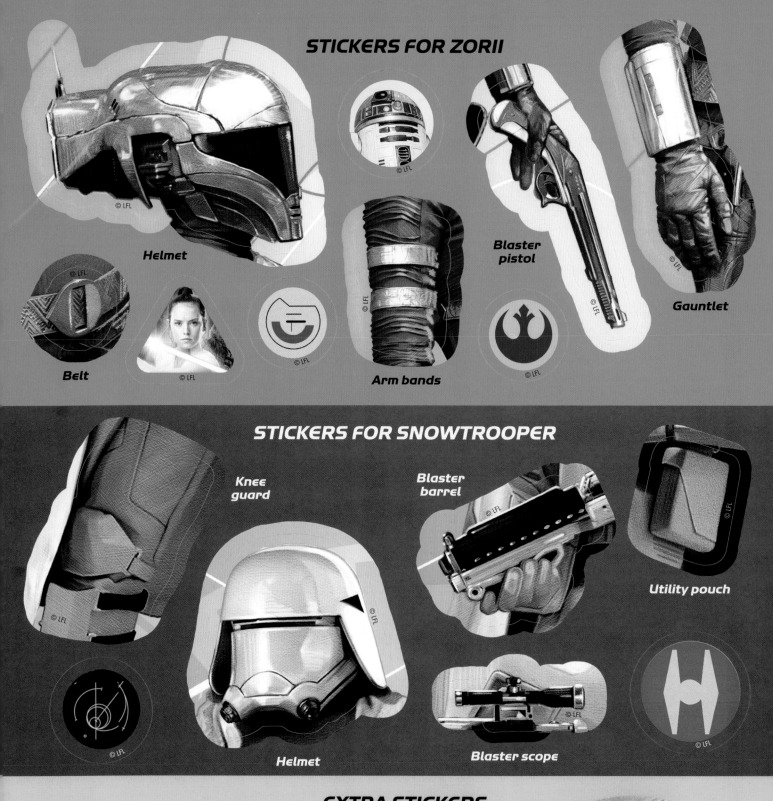

Helmet

Belt

Arm bands

Blaster pistol

Gauntlet

STICKERS FOR SNOWTROOPER

Knee guard

Blaster barrel

Utility pouch

Helmet

Blaster scope

EXTRA STICKERS

EXTRA STICKERS

STICKERS FOR LANDO

Colorful shirt

Styled hair

Cane

Holstered blaster

Cape

STICKERS FOR KNIGHT OF REN

Club staff

Gauntlet

Mud-splattered robe

Helmet

Thermal detonators

EXTRA STICKERS

EXTRA STICKERS

EXTRA STICKERS

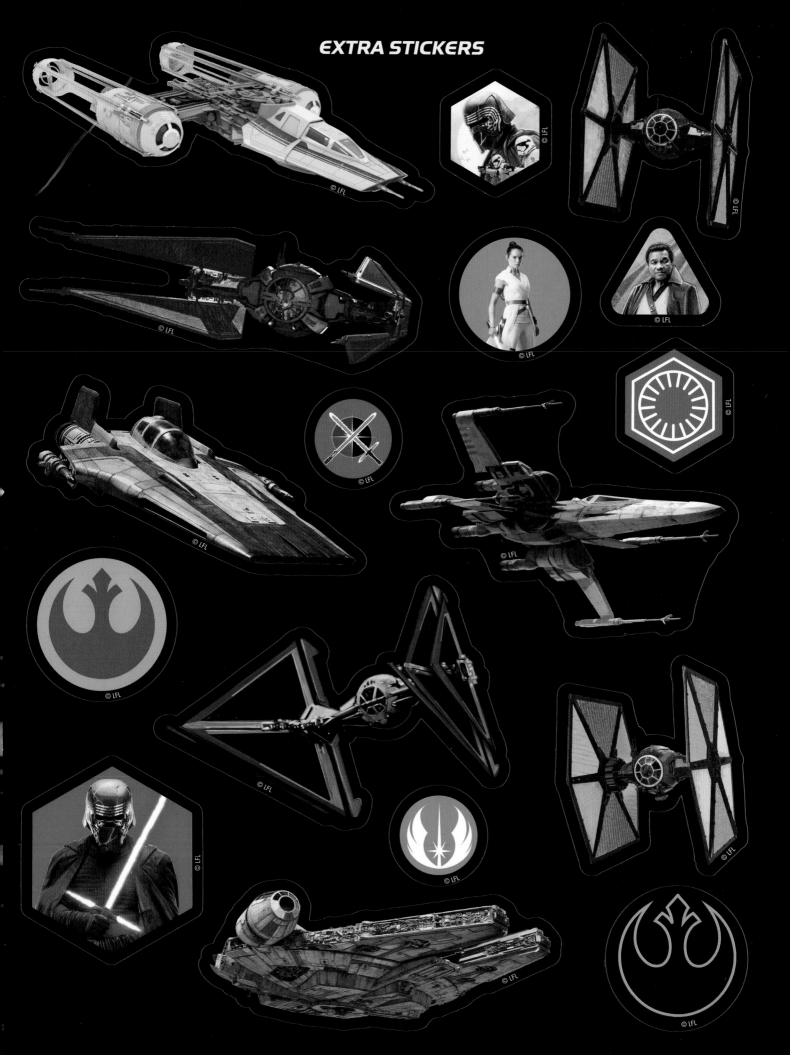